• • •

TO MY LOVING MOTHER
AND FATHER WHO INSPIRED ME TO
ALWAYS STAND UP AND WHO SHOWED
ME, BY THEIR BEAUTIFUL EXAMPLE, HOW
TO HELP OTHERS DO THE SAME.
—C. M.

• • •

TO MAYARIKA—
• • •
MY SUNSHINE, MY INSPIRATION.
—J. J. C.

• • •

Story adapted from "Get Up, Stand Up"
Written by Bob Marley and Peter Tosh
Published by Fifty Six Hope Road Music/Primary Wave/Blue Mountain (Irish Town
Songs ASCAP)/Campbell Connelly and Co Ltd/Reservoir Media Management Inc.
Illustration on pages 28-31 based on photo copyright © Fifty-Six Hope Road
Music, LTD.

• • •

Library of Congress Cataloging-in-Publication Data:
Names: Marley, Cedella, author. | Cabuay, John Jay,
illustrator. | Marley, Bob. Get up stand up.
Title: Get up, stand up / adapted by Cedella
Marley ; illustrated by John Jay Cabuay.
Description: San Francisco, California : Chronicle Kids, [2019] |
"Based on the song by Bob Marley." | Summary: Children are
encouraged to resist bullying and stand up for their rights.
Identifiers: LCCN 2018035377 | ISBN 9781452171722 (alk.
paper)
Subjects: LCSH: Bullying—Juvenile fiction. | Human
rights—Juvenile fiction. | CYAC: Stories in rhyme. |
Bullying—Fiction. | Human rights—Fiction. |
LCGFT: Picture books.
Classification: LCC PZ8.3.M39178 Ge 2019
| DDC [E]—dc23 LC record available at
https://lccn.loc.gov/2018035377

• • •

Manufactured in China.

• • •

Design by Alice Seiler.
Typeset in Mikado and Mrs. Lollipop.
The illustrations in this book were
rendered in pencil and digitally.

• • •

10 9 8 7 6 5 4

• • •

Chronicle books and gifts are available at
special quantity discounts to corporations,
professional associations, literacy programs,
and other organizations. For details and
discount information, please contact our premiums
department at corporatesales@chroniclebooks.com
or at 1-800-759-0190.

• • •

Chronicle Books LLC
680 Second Street
San Francisco,
California
94107

• • •

Chronicle Books—we see things
differently. Become part
of our community at
www.chroniclekids.com.

• • •

TUFF
GONG

Based on the song by

BOB MARLEY

GET UP, STAND UP

Adapted by
CEDELLA MARLEY

Illustrated by
John Jay Cabuay

chronicle books · san francisco

When you meet someone
talking big and thinking small,

and their stinging words
push your back against the wall . . .

No matter the silly games
that people play,

you have hopes and dreams
they can't take away.

When their words bite,
STAND UP for what's right.

Some people need to be
the pond's biggest fish.

They don't speak the truth
and only want their greedy wish.

Remember to be true,
the best of yourself.

Then you'll be a friend
to everybody else.

Don't just sit tight.
Be a **BRIGHT LIGHT.**

GET UP, STAND UP.
STAND UP FOR YOUR RIGHTS.

Other people parade around
with their noses stuck up in the air.

They strut about all puffed up
only thinking for what they care.

But if you know the value
of what life is worth,

you will find your feet
firmly planted on the earth.

Love with all your might.
BE TRUE to what is right.

Be a good neighbor and
cherish your sisters and brothers.

Practice being kind
to yourself and one another.

What you give in goodwill,
shall be returned back to you.

Share your truth and compassion.
Together there's much we can do.

So now we **SEE THE LIGHT**.
We're gonna stand up for our rights.

GET UP, STAND UP.

STAND UP FOR YOUR RIGHTS.

GET UP, STAND UP.

DON'T GIVE UP THE FIGHT.

"GET UP, STAND UP, STAND UP FOR YOUR RIGHTS! GET UP, STAND UP, DON'T GIVE UP THE FIGHT!"

Standing up for yourself, standing up for others, and standing up for what is right are three very important values my parents instilled in my siblings and me when we were growing up in Jamaica. And as a mom of three sons, I felt it was important to pass this message of strength, compassion, and equality on to them.

It was important for them to know that not every day would be an easy day. Not every person they met would be a best friend and not everything would go their way, but they had to have the strength and courage to stand up for themselves when someone wasn't treating them with respect. It was also important for them to know that they must stand up, not only for themselves, but for others when they saw someone in need or in harm's way.

Adapting this song into a book for children was an emotional decision for me. It is a song that became an anthem for all those who struggle, a song that became a call for change with a message that continues to inspire everyone who hears it. With this book, I hope we've succeeded in bringing this message to readers in a different form, and that it also inspires them to do the right thing, no matter how hard that might sometimes be.

— Cedella Marley

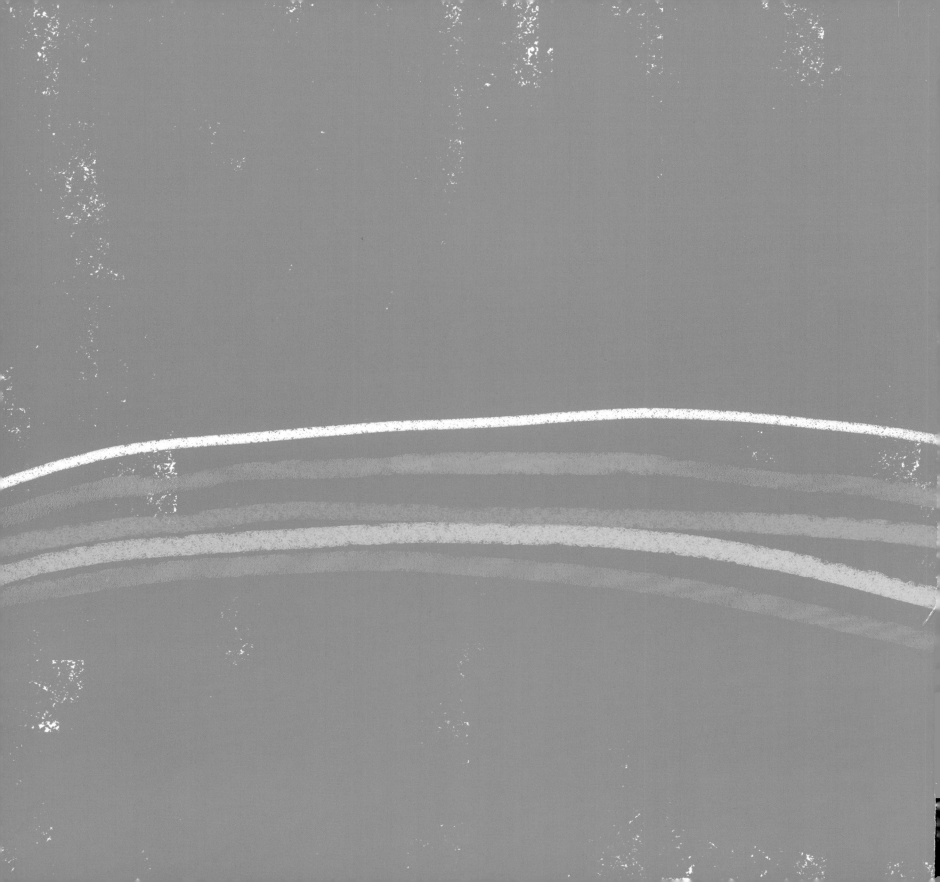